**When he** ▓▓▓▓▓
**he could hard** ▓▓▓▓▓ **his eyes. . . .**

Something very strange had happened in the photograph. The staircase wasn't empty. Climbing the stairs were two shadowy figures clothed in loose, white, hooded robes. Above the figures was a radiant white light.

The photo was examined by some of the top photographic experts in the country. No evidence of trick photography or any other kind of fakery could be found. There seemed to be only one explanation . . . ghosts.

**Other Apple Paperbacks
you will enjoy:**

# 13 GHOSTS:
### Strange but True Stories

# Will Osborne

AN
**APPLE**
PAPERBACK

SCHOLASTIC INC.
New York Toronto London Auckland Sydney

No part of this publication may be reproduced in whole or in part, or stored in a retrieval system, or transmitted in any form or by any means, electronic, mechanical, photocopying, recording, or otherwise, without written permission of the publisher. For information regarding permission, write to Scholastic Inc., 730 Broadway, New York, NY 10003.

ISBN 0-590-41690-1

Copyright © 1988 by Will Osborne. All rights reserved. Published by Scholastic Inc. APPLE PAPERBACKS is a registered trademark of Scholastic Inc.

12 11 10 9 8 7 6 5 4                    0 1 2 3/9

Printed in the U.S.A.                    01

First Scholastic printing, October 1988

*For Mary*

# CONTENTS

# 1

# The Ghost
# Who Carried a Coffin

Lord Dufferin couldn't sleep.

It wasn't the fact that he was away from home. His work as a British diplomat had taken him all over the world, and he was used to sleeping in strange beds. In fact, he felt quite comfortable in the huge, castlelike home of his Irish friend. But for some reason, even though it was very late and he was very tired, sleep would not come. Finally, he got out of bed, slipped on his robe, and walked over to the window.

The night was clear and the dew-covered lawns of the estate shimmered under the light of a full moon. It was a beautiful sight, and Lord Dufferin began to relax as he stood gazing out into the peaceful night. He was almost ready to go back to bed when he saw the strange little man stagger out of the shadows near the hedge.

Lord Dufferin watched as the shadowy figure trudged into the moonlight and began struggling across the lawn. The man was staring intently at the ground, and on his back was a big black box. The box was obviously very heavy, for it seemed to be all the little man could do to carry it without falling over.

Lord Dufferin wondered what could be inside the box. The man was clearly headed toward the house with it, but why? Perhaps he was making a delivery of some kind, but so late at night? And why did he insist on carrying such a heavy load alone?

On and on the little man struggled with his burden until he was standing directly beneath Lord Dufferin's window. Still staring down at the ground, he caught his breath and shifted the box on his back. Then he turned his face up toward the window and Lord Dufferin stepped back in horror.

The man had the face of death. His eyes were sunk so deeply in their sockets they looked like two black holes. His skin was as pale as the white lace curtains around Lord Dufferin's window. The moonlight clearly illuminated his sharp, pointed nose, his sunken cheeks, and his rotten, yellow teeth. It was a face Lord Dufferin knew he would never forget.

The man fixed Lord Dufferin in his gaze

for a long moment, then turned away from the house. He struggled back across the lawn toward the hedge and disappeared again into the shadows.

Lord Dufferin stood frozen, staring out at the silent lawn. Now he knew what the little man had been carrying on his back. The moonlight had lit it clearly as he walked away from the window. Lord Dufferin's heart began to pound. The box was a coffin.

"Well, old fellow, that's quite a story, but I can assure you there are no ghosts here!" Lord Dufferin's host poured himself another cup of tea. "And no little men delivering coffins in the middle of the night, either. Perhaps you fell asleep, dreamed you couldn't fall asleep, then dreamed you fell asleep after all!"

The other guests at the breakfast table laughed. "Perhaps Lord Dufferin is trying to scare us all away so he can have your estate to himself for a while!" said one. "For I am sure he is the last person here to believe in ghosts!"

Lord Dufferin smiled and shook his head. It was true: He didn't believe in ghosts. Still, he knew what he had seen. And he knew he hadn't been dreaming. Maybe someday he would understand what it meant. . . .

* * *

"I'm sorry, sir, the Paris elevators are a bit slow." The hotel manager looked anxiously around the lobby. "And we're terribly crowded this morning because of your diplomatic conference. I'm sure it will be here soon."

Lord Dufferin nodded and looked at his watch. The meeting was scheduled for ten o'clock sharp on the fifth floor. It was already five past ten, and the lobby was still crowded with people waiting to get upstairs. Lord Dufferin hated being late, but there was nothing he could do.

"Give me the notes for my speech," he said to his secretary. "We might as well go over them while we wait."

Lord Dufferin's secretary fumbled in his briefcase for the notes, and the two men began discussing the points the ambassador intended to make in his address to the other diplomats. They were deep in conversation when the elevator finally arrived and opened its doors.

"Sir?" The hotel manager tapped Lord Dufferin on the shoulder. "Better hurry, sir. You don't want to be left behind."

Lord Dufferin looked up from his notes to see that the elevator had already filled with people and the operator was about to close the doors. "Oh, yes," said Lord Dufferin, shuffling his papers. "Coming. Sorry."

Lord Dufferin hurried toward the crowded elevator, mumbling his apologies to the other passengers. He turned to the uniformed operator and was about to thank him for waiting when suddenly he stopped.

Lord Dufferin stepped back. A sharp chill ran through his body. He turned ghostly pale and his pulse began to race. Unable to speak, he grabbed his secretary's arm and gestured frantically for the elevator to go on without them. The doors closed and Lord Dufferin took a deep breath. He turned to the hotel manager.

"Who . . . who was that man?" he said, his voice shaking. "The man in the uniform operating the elevator?"

The hotel manager shook his head, puzzled by Lord Dufferin's strange behavior. "Why, I don't really know, sir. Our regular man is out today; we hired that gentleman as a temporary replacement. Why do you ask? Do you know him?"

Lord Dufferin never answered. Before he could speak, a terrible clanging came from the direction of the elevator. The manager rushed toward the closed doors as a series of loud bangs echoed through the lobby. There was an ear-piercing screech of metal scraping metal, then finally a crash that shook the whole hotel.

No one in the lobby spoke a word as the

noise of the crash died away. There was only one explanation for what had happened, and everyone knew what it was. The elevator's steel cable had snapped, and now the operator and all his passengers lay dead at the bottom of the shaft.

Lord Dufferin looked up at the floor indicator above the elevator doors. The arrow was frozen a little to the left of the number five. The cable must have broken just before the elevator reached the fifth floor, the floor where his meeting was to take place. Had he gotten on the elevator, Lord Dufferin would never have attended that meeting, or any meeting, ever again.

But Lord Dufferin didn't get on, for one reason. When he saw the elevator operator's face, he recognized it as the face he had seen from his window the night he couldn't sleep; the face of the deathly little man with the heavy black box: The Ghost Who Carried a Coffin.

Many people have premonitions of danger, but few are as dramatic as the events in this case. The facts were reported in the local papers, and the British Society for Psychical Research recorded the case, but Lord Dufferin was never able to discover the elevator operator's name, or anything else about him. His grandson has stated that Lord Dufferin, though he never believed in ghosts, always insisted that the story was perfectly true.

# 2

# The Curse
# of the Mummy's Bone

Sir Alexander never understood why his wife, Zeyla, stole the bone.

The year was 1936. The Setons were having a pleasant enough vacation in Egypt, seeing all the sights popular with tourists: the Great Pyramids, the Sphinx, the ancient ruins of the temples. And then one day their guide took them to a secret mummy's tomb not yet open to the public.

The tomb was buried deep in the earth, and the air smelled stale and musty as Abdul led the couple down the crumbling stone steps. "There are many here," the guide whispered, "but I will show you one that is special. She is my favorite."

The guide led the Setons to a stone slab. Sir Alexander felt a chill as his eyes grew accustomed to the dark. Lying before him on the ancient stone was the body of a young woman. She was partly wrapped in a rotting shroud.

Sir Alexander stared in horror at the mummy for a moment, then turned to go. He was eager to get back to the fresh air outside. "Thank you, Abdul," he said and started back up the stairs to the sunshine.

Abdul and Zeyla followed Sir Alexander up the steps, but when they reached the top, Zeyla touched Sir Alexander's arm. "Just one more look," she said. "Wait for me." And she hurried back down into the tomb.

Back in their hotel room, Sir Alexander was shocked when Zeyla showed him the small heart-shaped bone from the mummy's spine. "I stole it," she whispered. "I wanted a souvenir."

It was when Sir Alexander and Zeyla returned to their home in Edinburgh, Scotland, that the curse seemed to begin. They were saying good-night to their dinner guests. Everyone had enjoyed the party, especially the stories about the Setons' trip and Zeyla's theft of the bone. Sir Alexander had put the bone on display in a glass case in the dining room, and everyone had laughed when Zeyla told the story of sneaking back down into the tomb.

Sir Alexander was shaking hands with the last of the guests when suddenly he heard a loud crash over his head. He jumped back and a huge piece of the stone roof crashed to the ground beside him. Had it struck him, he would have been killed on the spot.

Sir Alexander tried to put the incident out of his mind. After all, he thought, it had been a windy night, and accidents happen. Still, something about the evening made him uneasy. Then the noises began.

Miss Clark, the Setons' nanny, heard them first: crashes and bangings coming from the dining room a few nights after the party. Sir Alexander heard them, too, and in the morning he found the table with the glass case overturned and the mummy's bone lying on the floor. It was getting harder to stay calm.

"Yes, Uncle, I saw it last night when I came down to the lavatory. A funny-dressed person, going up the stairs. Who do you think it could have been?"

Sir Alexander felt his heart begin to pound. He had almost grown used to the noises; they had been going on for nearly a month. But no one had seen a ghost — until now. Could the strange clothing his nephew described be a mummy's shroud?

"I . . . I don't know who it was," he said to the boy. "But I'm sure it's nothing to worry about. Run out and play, now. . . ."

* * *

Sir Alexander sat staring at the bone in its glass case. He had moved it upstairs to his study, locked all the doors and windows, and now he was waiting for something to happen.

The clock struck midnight, and still Sir Alexander waited. Everything was quiet. Sir Alexander began to feel a little foolish. But still he sat, waiting. The clock struck one.

Finally, Sir Alexander rose from his chair. He walked over to the mahogany table and looked down at the bone. This is ridiculous, he thought. The bone was just that: a bone, a little piece of a dead person's skeleton. It wasn't haunted, and ghosts existed only in the imaginations of little boys. He decided to lock up the room and go to bed.

Sir Alexander had been asleep only a few minutes when Zeyla woke him with her shouting. "Alexander!" she cried. "Alexander, wake up! Someone is in there! I heard them! Wake up!"

Miss Clark met the couple in the hall. "Did you hear it, sir?" she asked as they ran down the corridor toward the study. Her voice was trembling. "What is going on?"

Sir Alexander pushed the nanny aside and, taking his pistol from his robe, he unlocked the door and swung it open. The nanny screamed and Zeyla clutched at her chest. Sir Alexander looked around the room in complete astonishment.

The chair where he had sat to watch the bone was turned upside down. A heavy antique vase lay shattered on the carpet. Books were thrown everywhere. None of the furniture was where it had been when Sir Alexander left the room to go to bed. There was only one thing that had not been broken, upset, or moved. In the center of the room, lit by the moonlight from the window, sat the mahogany table; on the table was the glass case; and inside the case, untouched, was the mummy's bone.

After that, things got worse. No matter where Sir Alexander put the bone, it seemed to cause trouble. He moved it downstairs to the sitting room and came home to find the glassware shattered and the furniture overturned. He moved it back upstairs to the table in the study, and the table exploded, dumping the bone onto the floor. He moved it to a table in the dining room, and during a dinner party, that table hurled itself across the room and smashed into the opposite wall. Two women fainted, and the party was ruined. He loaned the bone to a newspaper reporter, and two weeks later the reporter fell terribly ill and had to be rushed to the hospital for emergency surgery. Sir Alexander decided he had had enough.

The kitchen was deadly quiet as Sir Alexander stoked the fire. Miss Clark, the nanny, pulled her shawl tighter around her shoulders. Sir Alexander's uncle stood holding the bone in both hands, eyes closed, his thin lips moving in a silent prayer.

Sir Alexander put down the poker and looked up at his uncle and Miss Clark. He wondered if Zeyla would ever forgive him for destroying her precious souvenir. "I am ready," he said softly.

Sir Alexander's uncle knelt beside him and slid the little bone onto the hot coals of the kitchen fire. A thin circle of flame surrounded it. The bone began to smoke, and then to burn with a dull red glow. No one seemed able to take their eyes away from the sight of the smoldering bone. They all watched until, finally, there was nothing left in the grate but ashes.

Unfortunately for Sir Alexander, burning the bone did not mean freedom from its curse. Surprisingly, Zeyla *didn't* forgive him for destroying her souvenir and the couple were divorced in 1939. Zeyla grew ill and died quite young after several years of poor health. Sir Alexander remarried twice but

remained depressed and unhappy. He felt his life had been ruined, and to his dying day he blamed his troubles on one thing: The Curse of the Mummy's Bone.

This case received a great deal of publicity in the newspapers of the time. It was investigated by the Edinburgh Psychic College, and Sir Alexander even attended one of their meetings to answer questions and report on the strange things that were taking place in his home. Some of the newspapers claimed the Setons were the victims of an ancient Egyptian curse, and printed letters from readers advising them on how to free themselves from the mummy's power. But no satisfactory scientific explanation was ever offered for the strange events that befell them after Zeyla stole the bone.

# 3

## The Phantom of the German Submarine

"Captain! Captain, he's there again! The second lieutenant! He's standing on the prow! Come see! Come see, quickly!"

The German commander of U-boat 65 glared at his sub-officer in disgust. He had no patience with the ghost stories the men were telling about his submarine — especially the story of the drowned second lieutenant who sometimes came back from the dead to walk the prow. But his officer was clearly upset, and the captain knew that sooner or later he would have to do something about the rumors.

"All right, Lieutenant," he said, pushing himself up from his chair. "Show me."

The captain followed his lieutenant through the submarine toward the observation deck. As the two men hurried through the narrow passages, the captain thought about the briefing he had gotten from Admiral Schroeder before he took command. It was true U-boat 65 had had some bad luck. Five workers had been killed during her construction in 1916: three from poisonous fumes that leaked into the engine room, and two more by a steel girder that fell mysteriously as it was being lowered into the hull. Then, during her first trials, an officer making a routine inspection of her hatches seemed to lose his mind; he walked overboard into the churning waters and disappeared forever. And when she was finally launched into active duty on the open seas, U-65's problems grew even worse.

The submarine's first official dive was almost her last. The ship sank to the ocean's floor and refused to surface. For over twelve hours she lay stuck at the bottom of the sea, terrifying the crew and the officers alike. The problem was finally traced to the batteries, but no reason was ever found for their malfunction. Rumors began to spread that the ship was jinxed. And the very next day an event occurred that made the rumors seem true.

The U-boat had been taken for inspection back to the Belgian port where it had been built. The engineers could find no problems, and the crew was preparing the ship to put out to sea again. Suddenly, there was a terrible explosion. One of the torpedoes on board had gone off — for no apparent reason. The blast killed five crewmen and one officer. The officer was a second lieutenant . . . and now the men were saying he had come back from the dead.

The captain pushed his way through the crowd that had gathered to see the ghost. This was the third time since the torpedo explosion that the ship's routine had been disrupted by reports of the second lieutenant's return, and the captain was eager to see for himself what the men saw, or *thought* they saw, that frightened them so. If someone is playing a joke, he thought, that someone is going to be in big trouble.

"There! There he is!" The sub-lieutenant's hand was trembling as he pointed toward the uniformed figure standing stiffly on the prow. "You see, Captain, it is him! Just like the other times! Always there in the same spot, staring out to sea with his arms folded! Folded across his chest — like a dead man ready to be buried."

The captain stared at the figure in disbelief. The sun was bright, the air was clear, and there was definitely someone — or something — standing motionless on the prow of his ship. The figure's face was turned away, but there was no mistaking the uniform as that of a German naval lieutenant. For the first time, the captain began to feel afraid.

The captain raised his hands to his mouth and shouted above the roar of the sea. "You, on the prow! Stand to! This is the captain!" The figure continued to stare out at the waves.

"You there! Identify yourself!" the captain called again, and slowly the figure began to turn toward him.

The face was young, but the eyes looked weary and sad. Fine wisps of blond hair blew from under the officer's cap, and the strong jaw and well-trimmed moustache made the face unmistakable. It was, without a doubt, the face of the drowned second lieutenant.

The captain gasped, then fumbled for the silver whistle around his neck. "Dive!" he shouted to the crew. "All hands get below and dive! Dive! Now!"

The crew flew into action and the submarine plunged beneath the surface of the sea. Some members of the crew heard an eerie laughter ringing through the U-boat's passages. The captain immediately put the ship on a course back to its base in Belgium. Perhaps he intended to recommend it be withdrawn from service; perhaps he merely wanted to give the crew a rest and some time to calm down. No one will ever know. When the submarine arrived at the port, an Allied attack was in progress. Before the captain even set foot off the boat, he was struck and killed instantly by an exploding bomb.

"I don't like it, either, but I have no choice." Admiral Schroeder dipped his pen in the inkwell on his desk and turned to the final page of the document his secretary had placed before him. "We're fighting a war, you know, and we're losing!" The admiral scrawled his signature across the bottom of the paper. It was 1918, and U-65 was being officially returned to active duty.

A year and a half had passed since the captain was killed by the bomb, and during that time the sub had gone out only once. But on that single tour of duty the ghost was seen again, and three of the men who saw it never returned. One died suddenly of a strange, unidentified fever. One fell overboard and was lost at sea. And the third went completely insane and took his own life.

Even the high officials in the German Imperial Command began to wonder if it might be best to scrap the jinxed U-boat once and for all. But Germany was suffering heavy losses in the war, and every available ship was needed for service.

Admiral Schroeder assigned a completely new crew and captain to the U-boat, and directed that the ship be fully inspected, repaired, and overhauled before she was put to sea again. In June 1918, she was judged fit and ready for service. The new captain launched her once more onto the open seas. Her orders were to patrol the Irish coast.

The American captain of U.S. Navy Submarine L-2 squinted through his binoculars at the German sub. It seemed odd that an enemy U-boat would surface so near the friendly Irish port of Cape Clear, but there she was, drifting silently on the calm waters. The lettering on the hull clearly read "U-65." The captain gave orders to approach the vessel with caution.

As the American sub motored slowly toward the German U-boat, the L-2's captain wondered if he might be heading into a trap. Perhaps the German sub was a decoy, sent to lure American ships close enough for a surprise attack. The captain called orders to stop the approach, then picked up his binoculars and peered at the U-boat again. He wasn't prepared for what he saw.

"Hey, take a look at this," he called to his chief ensign. "There's someone standing on the bow of that ship."

Suddenly, there was a blinding flash of light and the German U-boat was engulfed in a ball of flame. The force of the explosion rocked the seas, and when the smoke cleared, what was left of U-65 was sliding rapidly below the surface, never to be seen again.

No one ever found out what caused U-boat 65 to explode. But as the sub was going down, another American officer joined the L-2's captain and his ensign on the bridge. The three men watched through their binoculars as the German sub disappeared into the water, and all three saw the same bizarre sight.

Standing on the U-boat's prow was the figure of a German officer. He was dressed in a heavy overcoat and his arms were folded across his chest. They said he was smiling.

They were the last men ever to report seeing the Phantom of the German Submarine.

In the years since World War I, the case of U-boat 65 has been thoroughly investigated by ghost researchers and the German Navy as well. Since the U-boat was destroyed by the explosion, there is no record of her final voyage, and no explanation has ever been found for any of the other strange events connected with the submarine.

# 4

# The Ghost of the
# Yorkshire Museum

George Jonas first saw the ghost on Sunday,
September 20, 1953, at 7:40 in the evening.

Jonas was caretaker of the Yorkshire Museum in York, England. Sunday was not a
regular working day for him, but a religious
group had held a meeting in the big room on
the first floor that night, and Jonas had to
be there to lock up. The meeting was over,
the group had left, the doors were locked,
and Jonas was down in the kitchen getting
ready to go home when he heard the footsteps upstairs.

"It must be Mr. Wilmott," Jonas said to
his wife. Wilmott was the museum's direc-
tor, and Jonas thought perhaps he had come
to take care of some business in his office
while the museum was closed to the public.

"I'll go up and tell him we're going home,"
Jonas said. He was halfway up the stairs to
the offices when he saw the little man.

The man looked like an eccentric professor. He was dressed in old-fashioned clothes and had bushy white sideburns. Muttering softly to himself, he bustled out of Mr. Wilmott's office at the top of the stairs and headed across the hall. He didn't seem to notice Jonas at all.

At first, Jonas thought the man had come to call on Mr. Wilmott with some museum business. But it was an odd time to call, since the museum was never open for business on Sundays. Besides, Jonas was sure he had locked all the doors after the religious meeting. Perhaps the man had attended the meeting and gotten locked inside the museum by mistake.

Jonas climbed to the top of the stairs and watched as the little man shuffled back across the hall and into Mr. Wilmott's office again. Whoever the man was, he had no business poking around by himself. Jonas went to the door of the office, but before he could speak, the man brushed past him and headed down the stairway.

"Excuse me, sir, are you looking for Mr. Wilmott?" Jonas called to the man's back.

The man didn't answer. He just kept talking softly to himself, repeating the same phrase over and over as he hurried down the steps: "I must find it; I must find it; I must find it. . . ."

Jonas followed the little man into the museum's library. The lights were off, but the man didn't seem to mind the darkness as he bustled down the aisles. Switching on the lights, Jonas found him in front of one of the tall bookcases pulling one book after another from its place on the shelves.

Jonas had had enough of the man's strange behavior. He thought perhaps the man might be deaf, so instead of speaking to him again, he reached out to tap his shoulder. That was the moment Jonas realized he had been watching a ghost.

The book the man had been holding fell to the floor, and George Jonas found himself staring at nothing at all. The little man had disappeared into thin air.

After that, the ghost behaved almost as if he had a monthly appointment at the museum. It seemed that every fourth Sunday he did something to make his presence known, always at 7:40 P.M.

Four weeks after his first experience with the little gentleman, George Jonas saw him again. It was after another of the religious meetings, but this time Jonas didn't mistake the man for an eccentric professor or someone there to meet with Mr. Wilmott. After he came downstairs from the offices, the ghost walked directly into the library —

through the closed wooden door.

The following month, again exactly four weeks later, Jonas and a friend went into the library after one of the meetings to look for the ghost. As they walked among the shelves, both men heard the sound of pages being turned, then the sound of a book falling to the floor. The two men raced to the center aisle of the library to find one of the books lying on the floor where it had fallen, its pages still moving. Jonas picked up the book and looked at the title. The book was called *Antiquities and Curiosities of the Church*. It was the same book the ghost had dropped before.

George Jonas began to worry about his sanity.

It was almost 7:40 P.M., four Sundays later, and this time Jonas felt he was ready for the ghost. He had assembled a group that included his doctor, his brother, a newspaperman, a lawyer, and two other friends. All had agreed to keep watch with him. If these men saw what Jonas saw, no one could call him crazy.

The seven men gathered at the museum's library at the appointed time. The bookcase and the book itself were thoroughly examined for any signs of trickery. Then all the men were assigned to posts around the library to wait for the ghost to appear.

George Jonas's brother James took his assigned seat at the end of the bookshelf and looked at his watch. James didn't believe in ghosts, and he didn't believe his brother's stories about the little old gentleman. He was willing to sit with the other men, though, if only to prove to George that the ghost existed only in his imagination. He hoped it wouldn't take too long.

The room was silent except for the ticking of the men's watches. It was well past 7:40 now, and no ghost had appeared. James was sure he was wasting his time. Then one of the books began to move.

James stared at the bookcase in astonishment as the book slowly eased itself from its place on the shelf. It slid forward until it extended well over the edge, hung there silently for a moment, then toppled to the floor with a thud.

James leaped from his chair and ran to the spot where the book lay on the floor, its pages still fluttering. It was the same book that had fallen twice before, the book the men had carefully examined for wires or threads when they arrived at the museum.

The other six men ran to the bookcase and the doctor examined the shelf with his flashlight. There was no trace of anything on the shelf or on the book itself that suggested trickery. And when the book fell, all the men in the room were at least five feet away. George Jonas felt he had proved his point.

George's brother James was still staring dumbly at the bookcase. George put his hand on his brother's shoulder. "Now maybe someone will believe me," he said softly.

The ghost never came to the library again. Four Sundays later, George Jonas was ill and unable to be at the museum, so Mr. Wilmott agreed to come in and watch the library alone. Nothing happened. The following month, a team of professional investigators got permission to take over the library and watch for the ghost, along with George Jonas and his brother. Again, nothing happened. But the ghost had gotten quite a lot of publicity, and for a while large crowds gathered outside the museum every fourth Sunday evening, waiting to hear any news of his reappearance.

No news ever came. Perhaps all the publicity had frightened the ghost away, or perhaps he had simply found what he was looking for on one of his earlier visits. But he was gone, and George Jonas's life went back to normal. Still, Jonas would never forget those months in 1953 when all he could think about was the little gentleman in old-fashioned clothes, searching so desperately for something on the library's shelves: The Ghost of the Yorkshire Museum.

This is a world-famous case that was thoroughly investigated by serious researchers interested in ghostly phenomena, as well as by the newspapers of the day. Some of the researchers believed that George Jonas was merely hallucinating when he saw the ghost, and that even though no evidence of such trickery was ever found, the book could have been pulled from the shelf by a thin thread. But George Jonas never changed his story, and the statements made to the press by the men present when the book fell from the shelf all indicate that they believed they had witnessed something supernatural.

# 5

# The Ghost
# of the Irish Bride

If the boy hadn't screamed, the nursemaid would have been sure she was dreaming.

She'd heard the stories about old Kinsale Fort and its ghost, of course. Some of her friends had even tried to talk her out of accepting the position there as governess for the new officer and his family. But good jobs for young women were hard to come by in the little Irish seaside port, and the nursemaid was skeptical about the ghost stories, anyway — until she saw the White Lady for herself.

Both the children had fallen asleep hours before, but the nursemaid was wide awake. She didn't mind sharing a bedroom with the little boy and girl. It was part of the job, of course, but she loved the children; and the soft, regular sound of their breathing as they slept made her feel peaceful and happy. She looked over at the two little beds and smiled.

Then something in the far corner of the room caught her eye.

The figure of a young woman was gliding silently toward the children. She was all in white, and her dress looked like an old-fashioned bridal gown. Her face and her hands were as pale as the white flowers on her dress. There was no door on the side of the room she had come from, and she made no sound at all as she moved across the floor.

The nursemaid was too frightened to move. She watched, terrified, as the woman in white glided across the room and stopped beside the youngest child's bed. The little boy's arms were folded across his chest, and his covers were tucked tightly under his chin. The figure gazed down at the sleeping boy for a long moment, then slowly reached out her pale hand and laid it on the boy's wrist.

"Take your cold hand from my wrist!" the boy screamed. But even before he was fully awake, the woman in white disappeared into the air.

"It's true, sir, I saw her with my own eyes! And I was just as awake as I am right now. I don't think she wanted to hurt the boy, but he felt her hand, sir! Even before he woke up, he felt her hand!"

The young officer shook his head. Perhaps the stories about the White Lady of Kinsale Fort were true after all. Several of the officers who had been stationed there before him claimed to have seen her, and their descriptions were all the same: a pale young woman dressed in an old-fashioned white bridal gown. People said she was the ghost of the daughter of one of the fort's first governors, a Colonel Warrender. The young officer knew the story, and it was one of the saddest he had ever heard.

Colonel Warrender had been appointed governor of the fort shortly after it was built in 1667. He was very strict with his men, but he loved his daughter Wilful dearly. Wilful was engaged to marry a young gentleman named Sir Trevor Ashurst, and Colonel Warrender was very happy that his daughter had chosen such a fine young man.

Wilful and Sir Trevor were very much in love. They were married on a beautiful summer afternoon, and their wedding was a joyful, glorious celebration. Filled with their love for each other, the couple was taking a sunset walk along the fort's battlements when Wilful saw the flowers.

"Oh, look!" she exclaimed, pointing down the stone wall of the fort to the clump of unusual blossoms growing among the rocks far below. "Aren't they beautiful!" She squeezed Sir Trevor's hand. "I wish I could have them for my bouquet."

A young soldier from Colonel Warrender's regiment was patrolling the battlements that evening, and he happened to pass the young couple just as Wilful spoke.

"Excuse me, ma'am," the young sentry said. "I'm not supposed to leave my post, but if those flowers would make you happy, I'd be glad to climb down and get them for you."

"Oh, yes!" Wilful exclaimed, clapping her hands. "Thank you! Thank you ever so much!"

The soldier looked down at the rocks, then back at the newlywed couple. "Perhaps your husband could take my place on the watch for a moment, then, while I fetch some rope," he said. The soldier leaned his rifle against the stone wall and slipped off the jacket of his uniform. "It won't take a moment, sir, and I'm sure there's nothing to worry about, but I'd hate to get caught leaving my post."

"Certainly," said Sir Trevor, taking off his own coat. He slipped on the military jacket and took up the rifle as the sentry hurried away into the compound.

It wasn't long before the young soldier returned with a length of strong rope, and soon he was lowering himself carefully down the steep rocky wall toward the flowers. Sir Trevor began dutifully patrolling the battlements in the soldier's jacket, and Wilful giggled every time he passed stiffly by her on his rounds.

By then the sun had set over the ocean, and the evening was beginning to grow colder. As he walked the battlements with his rifle, Sir Trevor began to worry that Wilful might be growing too chilly in the night air. Promising to bring her a lovely bouquet as soon as the soldier returned, Sir Trevor persuaded his bride to go home and wait for him in their quarters inside the fort.

Sir Trevor tenderly kissed Wilful goodbye, then turned to peer over the battlements. He wondered what could be taking the young soldier so long. But it had grown too dark to see the rocks at the foot of the steep wall, and he knew that if he called out to the man he wouldn't be heard above the crashing of the waves.

It had been a long day for Sir Trevor, and he decided to sit and rest for a moment while he waited. Leaning his back against the cold stone wall, he listened to the sound of the waves and thought about his wedding day and his beautiful new bride. Before he knew it, he was fast asleep.

Sir Trevor hadn't been sleeping long when

Colonel Warrender came marching up the battlements on his nightly inspection of the fort. The colonel didn't recognize his son-in-law in the shadowy light, and when he saw the uniformed figure slumped against the wall with his rifle across his lap, he flew into a fury.

"Why aren't you walking your post, soldier?" Colonel Warrender demanded, but Sir Trevor didn't stir from his sleep.

"Answer me, sentry!" shouted the colonel, his anger mounting. Still Sir Trevor didn't stir.

Colonel Warrender's hand shook with rage as he jerked his pistol from its holster. "No guard sleeps on duty in my command!" he shouted and, aiming the pistol at the shining buttons of the sentry's jacket, he shot Sir Trevor through the heart.

When Colonel Warrender went to examine the body, of course, he realized his terrible mistake. Horrified, he immediately sent for the fort's doctor, but it was too late. Sir Trevor was dead.

Nothing could prepare Wilful for the terrible news that her father had killed her husband, and when she heard it, she became hysterical. Still dressed in her wedding gown, she ran to the spot where she and Sir Trevor had shared their last kiss. Seeing Sir Trevor's blood on the stones of the walk, she cried out in agony. Then, before anyone could stop her, she threw herself over the wall to her death on the rocks below.

Later that same night, unable to face a life of guilt and grief, Colonel Warrender locked himself in his quarters. With the pistol he had so foolishly used to make his daughter a widow on her wedding day, he took his own life.

Over the centuries, the ghost of the young bride in white has been seen many times. She has appeared in and around the rooms that Wilful was to share with her husband, and along the walk where the couple spent their last moments together. Sometimes she seems angry; usually, though, she only seems sad.

Perhaps on the night she reached out to touch the boy's wrist, she was merely yearning for the family she was never to have because of her father's foolish act of violence. On the day she died, she dreamed of becoming a wife and a mother; instead, she became the White Lady of Kinsale Fort: The Ghost of the Irish Bride.

The White Lady of Kinsale Fort is a case in which reported sightings of a ghost are explained by an old legend. There is no proof that the apparition is the ghost of Wilful Wallender, but it is interesting that all who have reported seeing the ghost over the years describe her in the same way: a young woman in white bridal clothes. The ghost has been seen by many reliable witnesses, including high military officials, and the case is considered to be one of the best examples of a consistently recurring apparition.

# 6

# The Ghost in the Brown Satin Dress

Captain Marryat thought the Brown Lady was beautiful.

As he got ready for bed that night, he had to admit her portrait looked a little more ominous in the flickering candlelight than it had in the bright light of day. But he certainly wasn't frightened, and he definitely didn't expect to meet the ghost.

Captain Marryat was part of a large weekend party staying at the beautiful estate called Raynham Hall in Norfolk, England. When he asked his hostess about the famous ghost of Raynham Hall that afternoon, Lady Townshend took him to see the painting that hung in the cedar-paneled bedroom on the second floor.

"So this is the famous Brown Lady of Raynham Hall," Captain Marryat had said, gazing at the portrait of the aristocratic young woman in the brown satin dress.

"Yes," said Lady Townshend. "My brother, Colonel Loftus, had that portrait painted a few years ago, in 1835. He thought he was the first to see her." Lady Townshend smiled. "Oh, he was terrified! But people have been seeing her around the estate for years."

Lady Townshend went on to tell the captain how Colonel Loftus had made a sketch of the ghost after his encounter with her and commissioned an artist to paint her portrait from the sketch. No one in the family had been able to identify the woman, so the portrait was titled simply "The Brown Lady" and hung in the room where she most often appeared.

"Everyone who sees her is absolutely terrified," Lady Townshend had said. And that was when Captain Marryat volunteered to sleep in the haunted room.

It was nearly midnight and Captain Marryat was getting undressed for bed when he heard a soft knocking on his door. Startled, he glanced up at the portrait, then took his pistol from its case. Checking to make sure the gun was loaded, he tiptoed to the door and waited. The soft knocking came again, and Captain Marryat threw open the door and jumped back into the shadows. But there was no ghost at the door, just the two young nephews of Lord and Lady Townshend.

"Excuse me, Captain," said one of the boys, peering timidly into the room. "I hope you weren't asleep."

Captain Marryat breathed a sigh of relief and tucked his pistol into the belt of his trousers. "Not at all," he said.

"I was wondering if you might give me your opinion of a new pistol I just bought," said the young man. "I'm thinking of using it tomorrow at the shooting party, and Father told me you were an expert on guns."

"Certainly," said Captain Marryat. "Where is it?"

"Just down the hall, in our room," the young man said. "Are you sure you don't mind?"

"Not a bit," said the captain and, after locking his own door, he followed the two young men down the corridor to their room.

Captain Marryat talked with the two boys in their room for a while about guns and hunting, and the three of them joked about the ghost of the Brown Lady and the captain's daring offer to sleep in the haunted room. Finally, they all agreed it was time to get some sleep, and the boys offered to escort Captain Marryat back to his room. "Wouldn't want the ghost to catch you all alone," one of them said, and they all laughed as they went out of the room together into the hall.

All three of them saw the figure at the same time. She was carrying an old-fashioned lamp and moving slowly and steadily toward them down the long, dark hallway. Captain Marryat thought at first that she might just be one of the other weekend guests. But the women in the party were all staying in another wing of the mansion, and besides, there was something very strange about the way the figure seemed to glide soundlessly along the corridor.

Captain Marryat and the two boys quickly ducked into the doorway of an empty room across the hall. As the figure came closer, Captain Marryat could see her dress clearly in the lamplight, and he felt himself begin to shake. The figure was wearing the same brown satin gown he had seen in the Brown Lady's portrait.

The figure continued to glide closer and closer until it was directly opposite the doorway in which Captain Marryat was hiding with the two boys. Then it stopped.

Lifting the lamp slowly to her face, the woman in brown turned and smiled wickedly at the captain. Though her features were the same as they appeared in her portrait, her expression was different: it was evil, and so full of hatred and malice that Captain Marryat was terrified for his life.

Pulling the loaded pistol from his belt, Captain Marryat leaped into the hall and fired point-blank at the figure. The silence was shattered by the shot, but the figure did not move. And the moment after the gun went off, she disappeared.

The two boys rushed across the hall and found the bullet embedded in the wooden door of their room. It had passed right through the figure's body, and the captain was left with only his smoking gun and the memory of the phantom's evil smile.

The captain stared at the bullet in the door for a moment, then looked down at his pistol. He knew he had just seen a ghost, and he would remember her face for the rest of his life. He would make no more jokes about the haunted room or the portrait of the aristocratic young woman that hung there: The Ghost in the Brown Satin Dress.

After that night the figure of the Brown Lady was not seen again for nearly a hundred years. Her portrait was sold at an auction in 1904, and at that time she was identified as Dorothy Walpole, the sister of England's first prime minister. Dorothy Walpole died at Raynham Hall in 1726, but the cause of her death is not known.

In 1926, the Brown Lady was seen by two boys on the staircase leading to her room on the second floor. Even though they had never seen the portrait and knew nothing of the story of the ghost, both boys described the phantom exactly as she appeared in the painting.

Ten years later, in 1936, two photographers were taking pictures of Raynham Hall for a magazine called *Country Life* when one of them claimed to see a ghostly figure descending the stairs. The second photographer quickly snapped a photo of the staircase, and when it was developed it clearly revealed the shadowy, transparent form of a woman in a long, flowing gown.

The combination of the photograph, the portrait, and the many different sightings of the Brown Lady over two centuries makes this case one of the most interesting in the history of ghost research.

# 7

# A Murder Solved
# by a Ghost

There was something wrong with the butler's story.

The burglary had occurred almost four months earlier, but as he lay in bed that night in the spring of 1730, Mr. Harris couldn't stop turning over the facts of the incident in his mind. Harris had been away in London carrying out his duties as a member of the Court of King George II when it happened, and his big country estate had been left in the hands of his butler, Morris. Morris had been with the family for nearly thirty years, and Mr. Harris trusted him completely. Still, there had been something odd about his report, and Mr. Harris couldn't put his finger on what it was.

Mr. Harris had gotten word of the burglary in an urgent letter from Morris only a few days after it happened. Rushing home from London, he found the butler upset over the loss and eager to tell his employer the full story.

"There were noises downstairs in the pantry, sir, in the middle of the night," the butler had said. "The noises woke me up, and I felt it was my duty to go downstairs and investigate. I was sure I had locked the pantry when I made my rounds before going to bed, sir, but when I got downstairs, there was a light shining from under the door.

"I put my ear to the door and heard the sound of men's voices whispering, then the sounds of wooden boxes being broken open. As you know, sir, we have always kept the family silver boxed up and stored on the pantry shelves when you are away."

Mr. Harris nodded and the butler continued.

"Well, sir, I knew we were being robbed, and I am ashamed to admit that I immediately suspected it was your two footmen. They were the only other men in the house, sir, and, foolishly, it didn't occur to me that the robbers could have broken in from outside.

"That was a terrible mistake, sir, as I soon found out. But at the time, the thought that members of your own household staff were betraying you so enraged me that I did something very foolish. Not thinking to call for help, I threw open the door myself and demanded to know what was going on.

"There were two men there all right, sir, but they were definitely not your footmen. I daresay you would never employ such a pair of brutal-looking thieves. They were evil-looking men, sir, and they were packing the family silver into bags while young Tarwell looked on."

"Young Tarwell?" Mr. Harris said, interrupting the butler. "Who the devil is young Tarwell?"

"Oh, sorry, sir, I'd forgotten you'd never met him. Richard Tarwell, sir, a lad of about fourteen from one of the local families. I hired him to help around the kitchen shortly after you left for London. The old kitchen helper had run off, and I thought Tarwell seemed a hard-working, honest lad. That was another of my mistakes, sir, as you will soon learn."

"All right," said Mr. Harris. "Go on."

"Yes, sir. Well. There they were, sir, the three of them, stealing your silver, and not very happy that I had caught them in the act. The bigger of the two men came at me with the iron bar they had been using to break open the boxes, and that was the last thing I remember, sir, until I woke up a little before dawn, gagged and tied hand and foot to one of the pantry chairs. The silver was gone, and so were Tarwell and the two men.

I looked around at the doors and windows to see where the thieves had broken in, and suddenly I realized that the whole thing had been planned."

Morris looked gravely at Mr. Harris. "Sir, young Tarwell must have been in on the plot from the beginning and *let* them in," he said, "for the doors and the windows hadn't been broken at all." The butler nodded significantly at his employer, then went on with his story.

"Well, there was nothing I could do, sir, but wait until someone noticed I was missing. Fortunately, it wasn't long before one of the footmen that I had so wrongly assumed a thief came looking for me, and as soon as he untied me I called the local police. But I'm afraid it was too late, sir. The silver is gone, and so are the men who stole it."

"And Richard Tarwell?" said Mr. Harris.

"Oh, he's gone, too, sir," said the butler. "Ran off that same night, as you might expect he would. His family claims not to have seen him since that night, either." The butler shook his head and looked out the window at the grounds of the estate.

"I'm sure we've seen the last of young Richard Tarwell, sir, forever."

A few days later, Mr. Harris was back in London carrying on his business at the

Court. The police had been of no help in locating the robbers, and Harris assumed the silver was gone for good. But he was a very wealthy man, and felt that the loss of a few pieces of silver was no great tragedy, particularly since no one had been seriously hurt in the robbery.

It was only when his Court business was completed and he returned to his estate four months later that the story of the young boy and the two thieves began to prey on his mind.

Harris lay in his bed, staring at the ceiling. The trip from London had been exhausting, but still he couldn't sleep. What was it about the robbery that was bothering him so?

He had heard the whole story again before going to bed as he followed Morris through the house on his nightly rounds. The butler was unusually conscientious, Harris noticed, in making sure all the windows were sealed and the doors locked from the inside.

"I say, Morris, are you always this careful with the locks?" Harris had said as the butler locked the final door and tucked the big ring of keys safely in his pocket.

"Oh, yes, sir," the butler had said. "Always." And Harris knew he was telling the truth.

But for some reason, Mr. Harris was troubled. I'll speak to Morris again in the morning, he thought, then rolled over and went to sleep.

The boy standing at the foot of his bed was Richard Tarwell.

Mr. Harris didn't know how he knew that, but he was certain it was true. He had known it the instant he awoke with a start to find the boy staring down at him in the dim light.

"What are you doing here?" demanded Mr. Harris, sitting up and pulling the covers around him, but the boy just continued to stare silently at him from the foot of the bed.

"Can't you talk?" said Harris. He wondered if the boy had been hiding out somewhere in the house since the robbery. Perhaps he wished to confess but was too frightened to speak.

Slowly the boy raised his arm and motioned for Harris to get out of bed. Then he pointed toward the door.

Harris thought he understood what the boy wanted. He got out of bed and, pulling on his boots and throwing a coat on over his nightshirt, he followed the boy out the door and into the hall. That was when he realized Richard Tarwell was a ghost. For though the boy was wearing heavy boots, his footsteps on the hard wooden floor made no sound at all.

Tarwell's ghost led Harris out of the house through a side door that was wide open, even though Harris had watched his butler, Morris, lock it securely only a few hours before. Then the boy walked silently across the lawn toward a huge oak that grew about a hundred yards from the house.

Harris looked on in amazement as the figure of the boy pointed down at the ground beneath the tree, then circled around to the far side of the huge trunk and disappeared.

Standing in the cool, starlit night, Harris stared at the spot on the ground where the boy had pointed, and he thought about the open door they had passed through to get outside. Suddenly, he realized what was wrong with the butler's story, and what it was that Richard Tarwell's ghost wanted him to know.

The next morning, the footmen found the body only a few minutes after they started digging at the base of the tree. Mr. Harris had shown them exactly where to dig, and he wasn't at all surprised when both men identified the body immediately as Richard Tarwell's.

Mr. Harris sent for the police and when they arrived, he called for Morris to follow them out to the oak. When Morris saw that the shallow grave had been dug up at the bottom of the tree, he fell to his knees and confessed his terrible crime.

The robbers had planned their theft that night with the butler, not the kitchen boy. Morris had let them into the pantry through the side door, and it had been Richard Tarwell, not Morris, who had been awakened by the sounds of the silver boxes being broken open in the middle of the night. Tarwell caught all three of the robbers in the act, and so they killed him. They buried his body beneath the oak, then Morris allowed himself to be tied and gagged so his version of the story would seem more genuine.

What had been bothering Mr. Harris about Morris's story was the matter of the key. The butler claimed Richard Tarwell had let the robbers into the pantry. But Morris would never have entrusted any of his keys to a kitchen helper, and he himself had said all the doors were locked on his rounds before he went to bed. It was unlikely that Tarwell would have been able to steal the large key ring from the butler's bedroom without waking him up, and besides, the butler had never mentioned that any of his keys were missing. But it was only when Tarwell's ghost led Mr. Harris through the mysteriously opened door and on to the site of his grave that Harris was able to put the pieces of the puzzle together.

Morris was tried for his crime, found guilty, and hanged. Mr. Harris testified against him at his trial, and the judge must have been surprised to hear the strange tale of how Richard Tarwell had helped to bring at least one of his own murderers to justice. It is one of the few cases on record of a Murder Solved by a Ghost.

This story can be found in its entirety in the transcripts of the trial of Richard Morris, which took place in Exeter, England, in the 1730s. At the trial, Mr. Harris swore under oath that his encounter with the ghost of Richard Tarwell took place just as it is described here.

# 8

# The Ghosts of the
# Tulip Staircase

Reverend Hardy stared at the photograph and shook his head. He clearly remembered the afternoon he had taken it. He was sure there had been no one climbing the spiral stairs when he clicked the shutter. But now, as he stared at the finished print, he could hardly believe his eyes. . . .

Reverend Hardy and his wife were on vacation in England when the photo was taken. It was the summer of 1966, and the Hardys were visiting the Maritime Museum in Greenwich. Reverend Hardy was eager to collect a few more snapshots of their trip before they returned to their home in Canada, and the historic old museum seemed the ideal place to do it.

The architecture of the Maritime Museum's buildings dated back to Shakespeare's day, and the Hardys were particularly impressed by a building known as the Queen's House. England's King James I had built it for his wife, Queen Anne of Denmark, and it was splendid in every detail. One of the features of the house that was most popular with tourists was the magnificent Tulip Staircase.

The Hardys gazed up at the long, curved stairs. The Tulip Staircase was truly a beautiful piece of work. An ornate pattern of sculpted tulips decorated its iron banister, and the steps themselves swept upward in a graceful arch. Reverend Hardy thought it would make a fine picture, and his wife agreed.

The museum was crowded with other tourists that day, but the Hardys decided it would be best to wait until the staircase was empty for their photo. They wanted to capture all the details of the ornate tulip railing and didn't want the picture crowded with people they didn't even know. Reverend Hardy got his camera ready and waited.

Finally, there came a moment when the staircase was empty. Reverend Hardy checked his focus, framed the shot in his viewfinder, and snapped the shutter. Satisfied that they had the photo they had been waiting for, the Hardys continued their tour through the museum. It was not until they were back home in Canada sorting through the prints that they realized something very strange had happened.

The Ghost Club was founded in London in 1862 to investigate people's experiences with the supernatural. Over the years, the club had developed a reputation for its meticulous research and thorough investigations of ghostly phenomena. They often received photographs from people who claimed to have taken a picture of a ghost. Most were obvious fakes: poor examples of trick photography submitted by people seeking easy publicity. But the photo Reverend Hardy sent them seemed different.

The Ghost Club's president held the photo up to the light. The staircase with its ornate tulip banister was clearly there, just as Reverend Hardy had framed it so carefully that afternoon in his viewfinder. But that wasn't the interesting part.

The staircase wasn't empty. Climbing the stairs were two shadowy figures clothed in loose, white, hooded robes. Their faces were hidden under their hoods, but their hands were clearly visible grasping the iron railing. One of the figures had a large, shiny ring on its finger, and above the figures was a radiant white light. The photo looked absolutely genuine, and Reverend Hardy didn't seem to be the kind of man who would merely be seeking publicity.

The president of the Ghost Club put down his magnifying glass and switched off the high-intensity lamp on his desk. "Well, it looks authentic to me," he said, turning the photograph over in his hands. "And this Reverend Hardy sounds like an honest fellow. He says here in his note he's never been interested in ghosts himself. Nice of him to think of us." He slid the photograph across the desk to one of the other Ghost Club researchers. "I say we send it out and let the experts have a look."

The Ghost Club sent the Hardy photo to be examined by some of the top photographic experts in the country. No evidence of trick photography or any other kind of fakery could be found. On their next visit to London, the Hardys met with officials of the club, who interviewed them extensively about their attitude toward ghosts as well as about the details of their trip to the museum on the day the photo was taken. The researchers all judged the Hardys to be reasonable, honest people, with no possible motive for trying to stage a hoax.

There seemed to be only one explanation. At the moment Reverend Hardy took his photo, the stairs were not empty at all. There were no tourists there and no employees of the museum. But there *was* a pair of ghosts: The Ghosts of the Tulip Staircase.

The Ghost Club was never able to duplicate the Hardys' photo with their own photographic equipment, even though they sent a team of investigators to the museum one evening to spend the entire night. They did, however, record the sound of footsteps, voices, and weeping in the vicinity of the stairs. And several of the museum's employees reported having seen "strange figures" around the museum for years.

As for the Hardys' photograph, it remains on file at the Ghost Club, and is still considered by many researchers to be the very best of the few unexplained ghost photos in existence.

# 9

# The Airman Who Flew Back from the Dead

"Hello, boy!"

Lieutenant Larkin jumped at the voice and the tap on his window. He looked up, startled, then he grinned. It was only his roommate, David McConnel. "Thought you were flying to Tadcaster this morning," Larkin said.

"I am. Forgot my map." McConnel pointed through the window to the crumpled map on his desk. "Could you hand it to me, please?"

Lieutenant Larkin passed the map through the window. He watched his friend hurry off toward the hangars, then went back to reading his paper.

The date was December 7, 1918, and World War I was finally over. Lieutenants McConnel and Larkin were both pilots in the British Air Force, sharing a room in the pilots' quarters of their home base in Scampton, England. Officially, McConnel was still only a trainee. He was eighteen years old.

McConnel's unexpected flight assignment that day was fairly routine. He was to deliver a single-seater plane called a Sopwith Camel to the airfield at Tadcaster, about sixty miles away. Another pilot would follow him there in a larger, two-seater plane called an Avro. Once the "Camel" was safely delivered, McConnel would fly back home with the second pilot.

The skies were fair that morning in Scampton. McConnel told his roommate, Larkin, he expected to be back in time for tea.

"The commander says we should use our own judgment," Lieutenant McConnel said, hanging up the phone. He grinned at the pilot of the Avro and looked up at the gray winter sky. "I think that means we go ahead."

The Avro pilot nodded and the two men pulled on their helmets and headed for their planes. They had been forced to land because of a sudden heavy fog, but from the ground, the fog didn't look too bad. And Lieutenant McConnel was eager to get his mission over with and get back to Scampton.

Once in the air, however, McConnel began to worry. The fog seemed to grow thicker with every mile. Finally, McConnel's partner was forced to bring the larger plane down again, this time in an open field.

Lieutenant McConnel circled the ground, trying to decide what to do. His arms were already tired from holding his little plane steady in the wind, and the fog was showing no signs of thinning out. But he was over halfway to the aerodrome at Tadcaster, and a forced landing in an open field might be almost as dangerous as continuing on.

On the ground, the pilot of the Avro was climbing out of his cockpit. McConnel flew his plane in low enough to see that the man wasn't hurt, then pulled back on the stick and headed off into the fog.


"Hello, boy!"

Lieutenant Larkin turned in his chair to see his friend McConnel grinning at him from the doorway. McConnel was still wearing his flying clothes but had exchanged his helmet for the naval cap he always wore around the base. He seemed in good spirits.

"Hello!" Lieutenant Larkin said, closing the book he had been reading. "Back already?"

"Yes," said McConnel. "Got there all right, had a good trip."

McConnel turned to go. "Well, cheerio!" he said and banged out the door.

Lieutenant Larkin settled back in his chair, found his place in his book, and went on with his reading.

That night the smoking room of the Albion Hotel in Lincoln was crowded with officers from the base. The air buzzed with the sound of their conversations as Lieutenant Larkin made his way toward the big stone fireplace in the corner.

Larkin hadn't seen his roommate, McConnel, since their brief conversation that afternoon. Another officer had come by the room later and suggested that he and McConnel might be going to Lincoln that evening, and Larkin expected he would run into the two of them there at the hotel. He set his drink down on the mantel and looked around the room for his friend.

A small group of officers was sitting at a table not far from the fireplace. One of the men was telling a story, and Larkin could tell from the other officers' expressions that the subject was a serious one. Curious, he lit a cigarette and leaned in toward the group.

Lieutenant Larkin couldn't make out exactly what was being said, but he did overhear the words "crashed" and "Tadcaster." He began to grow worried; and when he heard the man distinctly say "McConnel," he crushed out his cigarette and went over to the table.

"I'm sorry, but were you just talking about David McConnel?" Larkin said.

"That's right," the officer said, nodding sadly. "It's a shame. We got the word just before we left the base. Poor fellow."

"What do you mean?" Lieutenant Larkin said. "I saw him just this afternoon. He was in fine spirits."

The officer looked around at the other men at the table and shook his head. "I'm sorry, friend, but you didn't see David McConnel this afternoon. You couldn't have. He took a nosedive and crashed on the runway, trying to bring his plane into Tadcaster in the fog." The officer looked up at Lieutenant Larkin. "David McConnel was killed this afternoon."

It wasn't until the following day that Lieutenant Larkin was able to put together all the pieces of the story. And even then, he couldn't believe what had happened.

It was true. McConnel had crashed on his approach into the Tadcaster airfield. When the plane hit the runway, McConnel's head had struck the gun mounted in front of the pilot's seat. He was dead before anyone could reach him.

Lieutenant Larkin knew the approximate

time he saw his roommate for the last time. It had been between 3:20 and 3:30 that afternoon. That made the incident especially strange.

McConnel had been wearing a watch when his plane went down at Tadcaster. The watch was broken in the impact of the crash. The hands of the watch had stopped at the exact moment of McConnel's death. It was at 3:25 P.M.

Lieutenant Larkin would remember that afternoon for the rest of his life. He knew he was awake, and he knew without a doubt that the man standing in his doorway was his roommate and friend, David McConnel.

Perhaps the young lieutenant had come to say good-bye. Perhaps he didn't even know he had crashed. But David McConnel had definitely come home from his mission that day, if only for a moment.

He was the Airman Who Flew Back from the Dead.

This case is an example of what researchers call a *death coincidence*, in which a person at the moment of his death appears to a friend or family member in a distant location. All the details of the case were reported by

Lieutenant Larkin himself in a letter to McConnel's father, and the case was later investigated by a noted British ghost researcher. It is considered to be one of the best cases of this type on record.

# 10

# The Minister's Haunted House

She was there again.

Mrs. Smith peered out the window at the little woman leaning against the gate. She knew it would do no good to call out to her, or to go outside and say hello. She had tried that already, several times.

The first few times she saw her, Mrs. Smith thought the woman was a beggar, calling at the big house to ask for food. But when she asked the maid to bring her inside, Mrs. Smith got a strange response.

"Oh, no, mum, it's just the nun," the maid said. "I've seen her lots of times. Seen her carriage, too. She'll disappear if you try to talk to her."

The maid pointed out the window. "See that building out there? The Summer House? Old Reverend Bull built that back in the 1880s just so he and his son Harry could sit and watch for her. And you know that funny window in the dining room? Reverend Bull bricked it up because he didn't want her peering in at his family while they was eating. See how it faces that pathway by the roses? That's called the Nun's Walk. She's been coming around for years, mum, since the Middle Ages, I suppose, really, or whenever it was they killed her. . . ."

It was 1928, and Mrs. Smith and her husband, Reverend G. Eric Smith, had just moved into the big redbrick house known as Borley Rectory. The house had been empty for some time, and as soon as Reverend Smith accepted the call to go to Borley as minister of the parish, the Smiths began to hear rumors that the house was haunted. They paid little attention to the stories. That was their first mistake.

At first the disturbances were little ones. Mrs. Smith would hear the doorbell ring, go to answer it, and find no one there. Before she left the doorway, the bell would ring again, then all the bells in the house would start to ring. Keys that she left in their keyholes would suddenly leap from their locks and tumble to the floor. Lights would switch on and off in rooms that were empty. And there was also the matter of the skull.

It was a small skull, neatly wrapped in brown paper and tied up with string. Mrs.

Smith had been cleaning out one of the cupboards in the library when she found it. Once she got over the shock, she asked one of the workmen if he knew where it might have come from.

"Oh, yes, madam. I've seen this old relic before. It was around the house for quite some time. I always wondered if it was the nun's — from when she was alive, of course." The workman turned the skull over in his hands and ran his fingers through the hollow eye sockets. "Funny thing, though, madam," he said. "The last rector took it out and had it buried, years ago. I can't imagine how it found its way back."

It wasn't long after his wife found the skull that Reverend Smith began to hear voices in the house. At first they were only whispers: soft mutterings that sometimes were accompanied by heavy, dragging footsteps. Reverend Smith couldn't make out what the voices were saying, but they always seemed to be coming from just above his head, and they followed him no matter where he went. Then one evening he heard a single voice cry out in terror.

The voice began as a low moan. The moan grew louder and louder until it erupted into a chilling scream: "Don't, Carlos, don't!" It was the voice of a young woman, and she sounded as if she were pleading for her life. Reverend Smith heard her clearly as he was passing under the arch that led from the chapel into the house. But when he switched on the lights, there was no one there.

Reverend Smith took a deep breath. Was there to be no end to the strange happenings in his new home? He had never believed in ghosts, but at that moment he feared he would have to admit what people had been telling him all along: He and his wife had moved into a haunted house.

The Smiths moved out of the rectory in 1929. They never found out who Carlos was, or why their lights switched on and off, or if the skull Mrs. Smith found in the cupboard had belonged to the mysterious nun. Eventually they heard a local legend about a nun who had been murdered in a nearby monastery in the 13th century, but there was no proof that the legend had any basis in fact.

Still, many people thought it was the ghost of that unfortunate young woman that wandered the grounds of Borley Rectory, and sometimes galloped past the house in a phantom horse and carriage. They said it was her tortured spirit that caused the bells to ring and the lights to flicker on and off and the keys to jump from their locks. And even though no one really knows if the story of the murdered nun is true, to this day it remains as good an explanation as any for the strange events in Borley Rectory: The Minister's Haunted House.

The strange happenings at Borley Rectory have all been recorded as facts. Before the Smiths moved out, they reported their experiences to the London *Daily Mirror*, and the story attracted the attention of a famous British ghost hunter, Harry Price. Over the next twenty years, until his death in 1948, Price made Borley Rectory a major part of his investigative work. In 1940 he published a book that in its title called Borley Rectory *The Most Haunted House in England*. Later, a number of people criticized Price's work, but the mysteries of Borley Rectory remained unsolved.

The house was destroyed by fire in 1939, but the site itself remains a tourist attraction and the focus of continuing psychical research.

# 11

# The Ghost in the Rattling Chains

Athenodorous wasn't about to be driven out of his new house by a ghost.

His landlord had told him the house was haunted, and he had heard the stories of the men who went mad after spending a single night there. But the rent was cheap, Athenodorous was poor, and the house was exactly what the old philosopher had been looking for when he came to Athens to study and teach.

Athenodorous decided to move into the house despite the ghost stories, and he was determined not to be scared off even if the stories were true. "If there really is a restless spirit here," he said, "perhaps he will be good company for me."

Athenodorous chose to spend his first night in the house doing what he did every night: writing about his philosophy of life.

He prepared a study for himself in one of the rooms by spreading his notes and books out on a table. Then he cooked a simple dinner, ate it as the sun went down, and retired to his study to work.

The old philosopher wanted to put the ghost stories out of his mind, so that night he chose an especially hard philosophical problem to work on. He was deep in thought when a clanking sound in the distance interrupted his concentration.

Athenodorous paused for a moment to listen to the noise. It sounded as if heavy chains were being dragged along a stone floor. And the longer he listened, the closer the sound of the clanking chains came to his room.

The philosopher took a deep breath and went back to studying his notes. His work was much more important than his fear, he decided, and he was determined not to be shaken from it no matter what happened.

The sound of the rattling chains came closer and closer, but still Athenodorous sat thinking, writing, and studying his notes. He didn't look up, and he didn't give in to his fear. Finally, it sounded as if the chains were right in the room itself, and the clanking was too loud even for the strong-willed philosopher to ignore it any longer.

Athenodorous looked up from his work and a cold chill ran down his spine. Standing before him in the flickering light was the figure of a man — or what was left of a man. The figure was so thin he looked like a skeleton. His pale, gray flesh hung loosely on his bones and his long white beard was matted and filthy. There were shackles around his wrists and ankles, and attached to the shackles were long, rusty chains.

The figure glared at Athenodorous, and the look in his eyes was a mixture of rage and misery. Raising his frail arms above his head, he shook his shackles violently, and the sound of the rattling chains echoed through the dark and empty house. Then he motioned with his bony finger for Athenodorous to stand up.

Athenodorous was terrified, but still he didn't give in to his fear. He looked into the figure's eyes, shook his head, pointed to his work, then motioned for the figure to go away and leave him alone.

As Athenodorous went back to his writing, the figure began to moan in a broken, pained voice. The moaning grew louder and louder, and the figure shook his chains so violently that Athenodorous was forced to look up again. The expression on the ghost's face was one of pure agony. Again he beckoned for Athenodorous to stand up and follow him.

The old philosopher put down his pen and

stared into the ghost's pained, wretched face. Then, more in pity than in fear, he picked up his lamp and motioned for the figure to lead the way.

Athenodorous followed the ghost through the house and out the back door into the yard. The ghost dragged his chains to a clump of bushes in the garden, then turned to Athenodorous. He pointed down to the ground, shook his shackles one final time, then disappeared.

Athendorous took his lamp to the spot in the shrubbery where the ghost had pointed, but there was nothing there. He broke a few branches on one of the bushes to mark the spot, then went back into his house and went to bed.

"This is the spot," Athenodorous said to the city magistrate. "Tell your men to dig here."

Athenodorous had risen early the morning after his encounter with the ghost and reported the incident to the officials of the city of Athens. At first they refused to take the philosopher seriously, but Athenodorous was persistent, and eventually he persuaded them to follow him back to his house and investigate.

The magistrate's men uprooted the bush

at the spot where the ghost had disappeared. Then, as Athenodorous and the magistrate looked on, the men began to dig up the earth beneath the bush. It wasn't long before one of the men's shovels struck something hard, buried a few feet below the surface.

"Wait," the magistrate called to the men. Taking one of their shovels, he carefully cleared away the earth to reveal a shocking sight.

Lying in the shallow grave was a rotting skeleton, and Athenodorous knew as soon as he saw it that the skeleton had belonged to the man whose tortured spirit haunted his house. For there were shackles around the bones of the skeleton's wrists and ankles, and the shackles were attached to heavy, rusted chains.

Athenodorous had the chains removed from the skeleton's bones, and the poor man's remains were given a proper burial. After that, Athenodorous never saw the ghost again. Perhaps the dead man's spirit had merely been waiting for someone wise enough to meet him with kindness and pity instead of terror. Athenodorous did just that, and his house was never again haunted by the Ghost in the Rattling Chains.

This is the oldest ghost story in the book. It was recorded by Pliny the Younger in the first century A.D. Pliny was a respected Roman historian, and he reported the case to his patron as a true story.

# 12

# The Ghost with the Bright Red Scar

The young salesman was thrilled to see his sister, even though she had been dead for nine years.

He was sitting at the table in his hotel room in St. Joseph, Missouri, filling out the order forms from his morning's work. Bright sunlight shone through the window, and the young salesman was in a very happy mood. It had been a good day, and he was thinking about how pleased his boss would be when the home office received his list of new customers. He lit a fresh cigar and refilled his pen from the inkwell. Suddenly, he was aware he was no longer alone.

There was someone sitting at the table to his right. Startled, the salesman turned and found himself looking into the kind eyes of his sister, Annie.

"Annie!" the young man cried, leaping up to embrace her. But the moment he called her name, the pretty young woman disappeared.

The salesman stood staring at the empty space at the table where his sister had been. He had seen her clearly, and she looked exactly the same as he remembered her. But it was 1876, and Annie had died of cholera in 1867, nine years before.

As he stood in the empty hotel room puzzling over the experience, the salesman realized that he *had* noticed one thing that was different about Annie. Her features, her expression, the cut of her hair, even the way she was dressed seemed exactly the same as when she was alive. But her pretty face was marred by something he had never seen before. On her cheek, just below her right eye, was a bright red scar.

"I know it sounds crazy, Father, but I tell you I saw her! She was sitting as close to me as you are right now. And I'm sure I could go to her trunk in the attic now, Mother, and pick out the very dress she was wearing! I know it sounds impossible, but it's the absolute truth!"

The young salesman was sitting in the parlor of his parents' house in St. Louis. He had been so shaken by seeing his sister that he had cut his sales trip short and taken the next train home to tell his parents and his brother the story. At first, they were all skeptical.

"I think, son, that your mind must have been playing tricks on you," the young man's father said. "Perhaps there was something about the colors in the room or the kind of day it was outside that made you think vividly of her. Many things can suddenly stir the memory of someone you love."

"But it wasn't a memory, Father. Annie was there, in the room, with me!"

The young man's father just smiled and nodded, and the salesman could tell he didn't believe the story. Perhaps he should have kept the incident to himself, but seeing his beloved sister again after all those years had left him with a feeling of peace and happiness, and he wanted to share that feeling with the other members of the family that had loved her so much. How could he make them understand?

"I know you don't believe me, but I know she was truly there," he said. "And she was just as beautiful as I remember her. The only thing different was the scar."

The young man's mother looked up from her sewing. "The scar?" she said.

"Oh, yes, I forgot to tell you that. There was a scar on her cheek. It was more like a scratch, actually, for it was bright red, as if she had just scraped herself with a pin or something."

Suddenly, the young man's mother cried out in anguish and burst into tears. "Oh, my Annie," she wailed, and still sobbing, she told her family a secret she had kept from them for nine long years.

"It happened the morning of her funeral," the old woman said through her tears. "Annie was laid out in her casket and I was all alone with her in the room. She looked so beautiful lying there, so still. . . ."

The woman paused for a moment to dry her eyes, then went on. "But her hair . . . I always thought she looked so pretty when she wore her hair up, and I wanted to see . . . to see her like that one more time. I just wanted to pin her hair up, but my hand was shaking so badly . . . when I went to do it, I . . . I scratched her face." The woman covered her eyes with her hands and wept. "I scratched her beautiful face, and no one ever knew. I covered the scratch with powder and makeup before anyone saw," she said. "But all through the funeral I thought about it, and I've thought about it every day for the last nine years. You couldn't have known about that scratch unless you really saw her, unless she really did come to you. Oh, my Annie!"

The young man put his arms around his mother, and she cried for a while into the collar of his jacket as he stroked her gray hair. "It's all right, Mother," he said, looking over her shoulder at his father. "It's all right. She was happy, Mother, I could see it in her eyes. It's all right."

A few weeks later, the young man's mother died. She had not been well, and had she died before the young man told the story of seeing his sister, she would have taken the secret of the scratch on the girl's face with her to the grave. No one else in the world could have explained why the young salesman had seen the scar.

But when the old woman told her secret, even her skeptical husband was convinced that their son had seen a ghost. For one fleeting moment in a hotel room in St. Joseph, the young salesman had truly been reunited with his beautiful sister, Annie: The Ghost with the Bright Red Scar.

This case was reported to the American Society for Psychical Research in 1887. Their files are full of incidents in which people claim to be visited by the ghost of a deceased family member, but usually there is nothing to suggest that the "ghost" is anything more than a dream or a hallucination. The fact that the young salesman was unaware of the scratch on his sister's face at the time he claims to have seen her ghost sets this case apart, and makes it particularly interesting to researchers.

# 13

## The Revenge of the Murderer's Skull

Dr. Kilner had been thinking about the skull for weeks. Every day he went to the anatomy lab, just to look at it. And when he went home at night, he couldn't get it off his mind.

It wasn't an ordinary skull. It had belonged to one of the most famous murderers of the century, William Corder. Corder had been hanged almost fifty years earlier, in 1828, for murdering his fiancée on the night he had promised to marry her.

Thousands of people had come to the English village of Bury St. Edmonds that day to watch Corder die at the end of the rope. After the hanging, the hangman cut the rope into pieces and sold them as souvenirs. But Dr. Kilner intended to have the best souvenir of all: Corder's skull.

Corder's body had been donated to science after his hanging. His corpse was sent to a medical school, and eventually his skeleton wound up in the West Suffolk General Hospital, where it was used to teach anatomy. Dr. Kilner was a member of the hospital's staff.

To most people, all skulls look alike, and that was the key to Dr. Kilner's morbid plan. Late one night he sneaked into the lab where Corder's skeleton was kept. After making sure no one else was around, he carefully clipped the wires that attached the grinning skull to the skeleton's backbone. His heart pounding, he slipped the murderer's skull into his bag and replaced it with another skull he had stolen just for that purpose.

Dr. Kilner stepped back and looked at the skeleton. The moonlight shining through the window cast an eerie shadow of the murderer's bones across the floor, and a chill ran down Kilner's spine. But the new skull fit perfectly atop the skeleton's bony frame, and the doctor was sure that no one would ever know the original skull was missing. Grinning with satisfaction, Dr. Kilner grabbed his bag and hurried out of the hospital into the night.

A few weeks later, the servants began to complain. There were hammering noises in the drawing room, they said, and sometimes the sounds of sobbing. Doors were opening and slamming shut in the house for no reason. One day a man had come to call on Dr. Kilner, then vanished into thin air before the doctor arrived home. And some had seen the same man wandering around the house, then disappearing before they could even ask who he was.

Dr. Kilner locked the doors of the drawing room behind him and took the ebony box down from its special place on the bookshelf. My servants are all silly, superstitious people, he thought as he lit the candle on the table by the window.

Dr. Kilner sat down in his big easy chair and lifted the skull gently from the shiny black box. He ran his fingers over the bony jaw and gazed into the hollow sockets where the murderer's eyes had once been. No one at the hospital had any idea that Corder's skeleton had been tampered with, and Dr. Kilner felt a secret, smug pride as he turned the skull over in his hands.

The skull's surface had been polished to a high gloss, and Dr. Kilner had built the ebony box especially to house his prize. He treasured his grim souvenir and wasn't about to give it up because of his servants' silly superstitions.

Dr. Kilner put the skull back in its box, put the box back on the shelf, blew out the candle, and went upstairs to bed.

\* \* \*

There were noises coming from down-stairs. Dr. Kilner woke up with a start and lit the candle by his bed. It sounded as if there were someone moving around down in the drawing room.

"My skull!" breathed Dr. Kilner, throwing off his covers. The thought that someone might be stealing his prize possession sent him into a rage. He grabbed the candle and rushed out into the hall.

Dr. Kilner peered down the stairs at the pale, bony hand on the handle of the drawing room door, and his rage turned to stark ter-ror. For there was no arm attached to the hand, and no body. There was nothing there at all but a ghostly white hand, and the hand was about to open the door.

Before Dr. Kilner could catch his breath, the stillness was shattered by the sound of a terrific explosion inside the drawing room. The hand disappeared and the door blew open, smashing against the wall.

Swallowing his fear, Dr. Kilner ran down-stairs and into the room. The moment he stepped inside an icy wind swept over him, blowing out his candle and sending cold shiv-ers down his spine. Kilner groped in the darkness for a match, struck it, and what he saw in the dim light left him speechless with horror.

The ebony box lay in splintered pieces all

over the room, as if it had been blown apart by a terrific force. And staring down at him from the shelf, unharmed by the blast, was the grinning, bony face of Corder's skull.

After that night, Dr. Kilner knew he had to get rid of the skull. He also knew he couldn't put it back where it had come from, because the skull's polished surface no longer matched the bones in the rest of Corder's skeleton. He decided to give it away as a gift to the one man he could think of who might appreciate it.

F.C. Hopkins owned the old Bury St. Edmonds jail, the jail where Corder had been hanged so many years before. He had been an official of the Prison Commission, and when he accepted Corder's skull from Dr. Kilner, he didn't know what he was letting himself in for.

As he was carrying the skull home, Hopkins fell and sprained his ankle. But that was only the beginning of his bad luck. It wasn't long before the retired prison official found himself bankrupt, his personal life in a shambles, and his health gone.

Dr. Kilner's life was just as bad. He, too, had nothing but bad luck, and finally the two men decided to try to free themselves from the skull's power by giving it a decent burial.

Hopkins found a remote country graveyard far from his home, and offered the gravedigger money to find a peaceful resting place for the murderer's skull. The gravedigger agreed, and the skull was buried secretly in a quiet corner of the cemetery.

That may have been what the skull had wanted all along, for after that, things returned to normal for both Hopkins and Dr. Kilner. The rest of Corder's skeleton still hung in the anatomy lab, but perhaps his spirit had finally found peace. The ordeal was over, and no one ever again would suffer from the Revenge of the Murderer's Skull.

This case is similar to "The Curse of the Mummy's Bone" (p. 8). Both cases involve a series of strange events that seemed to occur as a result of disturbing the remains of a dead person. There are many superstitions that warn against violating the rights of the dead to rest in peace, but few cases on record which so clearly seem to verify the truth of these superstitions. No scientific explanation was ever found for the events in either case.

Pawnee Public Library

**APPLE'**PAPERBACKS

# Pick an Apple and Polish Off Some Great Reading!

### For Ages 11-13...

| | | | |
|---|---|---|---|
| ❏ | MU40321-4 | **Aliens in the Family** Margaret Mahy | $2.50 |
| ❏ | MU41685-5 | **Big Guy, Little Women** Jacqueline Shannon | $2.75 |
| ❏ | MU40267-6 | **The Computer That Ate My Brother** Dean Marney | $2.50 |
| ❏ | MU40849-6 | **Fifteen at Last** Candice F. Ransom | $2.50 |
| ❏ | MU40766-X | **Hurricane Elaine** Johanna Hurwitz | $2.50 |
| ❏ | MU41812-2 | **No Place for Me** Barthe DeClements | $2.50 |
| ❏ | MU42790-3 | **Our Man Weston** Gordon Korman | $2.75 |
| ❏ | MU41137-3 | **Still More Two-Minute Mysteries** Donald J. Sobol | $2.50 |
| ❏ | MU41052-0 | **The Summer of Mrs. MacGregor** Betty Ren Wright | $2.50 |
| ❏ | MU40323-0 | **Tales for the Midnight Hour** J.B. Stamper | $2.50 |
| ❏ | MU40589-6 | **With You and Without You** Ann M. Martin | $2.50 |
| ❏ | MU41637-5 | **You, Me, and Gracie Makes Three** Dean Marney | $2.50 |

*Available wherever you buy books...or use the coupon below.*

**Scholastic Inc.**
**P.O. Box 7502, 2932 East McCarty Street, Jefferson City, MO 65102**

Please send me the books al have checked above. I am enclosing $_____ (please add $2.00 to cover shipping and handling). Send check or money order — no cash or C.O.D.'s please.

Name _____

Address _____

City _____ State/Zip _____

Please allow four to six week for delivery. Offer good in the U.S.A. only.
Sorry, mail order not available to residents of Canada.
Prices subject to change.

AMM589

*Point*

# SCIENCE FICTION

Enter an exciting world of extraterrestrials and the supernatural. Here are thrilling stories that will boggle the mind and defy logic!

**OUT OF THIS WORLD**

## Point Science Fiction

- ☐ MH42318-5 **The Catalogue of the Universe**
  Margaret Mahy                                          $2.75
- ☐ MH40622-1 **Born Into Light** Paul Samuel Jacobs      $2.75
- ☐ MH41513-1 **The Tricksters** Margaret Mahy            $2.95
- ☐ MH41289-2 **The Changeover: A Supernatural
  Romance** Margaret Mahy                                $2.50
- ☐ MH41248-5 **Double Trouble** Barthe DeClements
  and Christopher Greimes                                $2.75

PREFIX CODE
0-590-

### More new titles to come!

Available wherever you buy books, or use coupon below.

**Scholastic Inc.**
P.O. Box 7502, 2932 E. McCarty Street, Jefferson City, MO 65102

Please send me the books I have checked above. I am enclosing $ _____ (please add $1.00 to cover shipping and handling). Send check or money order— no cash or C.O.D.'s please.

Name _____

Address _____

City _____ State/Zip _____

Please allow four to six weeks for delivery. Offer good in U.S.A. only. Sorry, mail order not available to residents of Canada. Prices subject to change.                    PSF1288